"That's ridiculou...
"Who'd be singin...
night . . . in the moonlight?"

"A-a-a g-g-ghost?" Carrie's voice quivered.

"There's no such thing as ghosts," Nikki quickly replied.

"Oh, yeah? Well, I've heard stories about ghosts—"

"*Shhh!*" said Ben. With one hand cupped behind his ear, he tilted his head and listened. The rest of the gang listened, too.

Then a grin slowly spread across Ben's face. He slapped his thigh and started to laugh. "I know what it is! It's the carousel! It's music from the carousel! Can you believe we let ourselves get spooked by *carousel music?*"

Carrie looked doubtful. "I never heard of a carousel running in the dark." She paused. "But if it *is* the carousel, that means there's someone there . . . and maybe that someone doesn't want company!"

THE CREEPY CAROUSEL

Lorraine Avery

Illustrated by Linda Thomas

Troll Associates

Library of Congress Cataloging-in-Publication Data

Avery, Lorraine.
  The creepy carousel / Lorraine Avery; illustrated by Linda
Thomas.
     p.   cm.—(Apple Park kids; 3)
  Summary: The Apple Park Gang decides to investigate when the
members hear ghostly music coming from the park's carousel and spot
some mysterious people lurking in the bushes.
  ISBN 0-8167-1712-5 (lib. bdg.)   ISBN 0-8167-1713-3 (pbk.)
  [1. Mystery and detective stories.   2. Clubs—Fiction.   3. Parks—
Fiction.]   I. Thomas, Linda, 1947-   ill.   II. Title.
III. Series.
PZ7.A952Cr   1990
[Fic]—dc20   89-20279

A TROLL BOOK, published by Troll Associates
Mahwah, NJ 07430

Printed in the United States of America.

10   9   8   7   6   5   4   3   2   1

THE CREEPY CAROUSEL

CHAPTER
ONE

"**H**old it! Don't move a muscle!"

No one moved a muscle.

Ben pressed the shutter. The camera clicked and whirred softly.

"It takes about a minute to develop," Ben said, tearing off the shiny white paper from the front of the camera.

Ben held the paper to the light as Nikki, Carrie, and Davey studied it. Slowly, three figures and a dog emerged on its surface.

"That's me!" Carrie cried, pointing to the girl in designer T-shirt and shorts.

"And me!" Nikki added.

Davey laughed and said, "Pitiful looks dead!" In the photograph, Davey sat between Nikki and Carrie. He was holding Pitiful, his basset hound. The hound's head hung limply over Davey's arm.

"That animal *always* looks dead to me," Carrie said, sniffing. She shuddered as she glanced at the real dog sleeping in Davey's arms. Carrie never tried to hide her dislike of dogs.

Ben tacked the photograph onto the clubhouse wall next to several others, then sat down next to Nikki. "I've only got five more shots," he said. "And it's my last roll of film."

Ben's father had given him the secondhand, self-developing camera and two rolls of film for his birthday.

"Dad was right. Photography *is* expensive. And the trouble is, I'm running out of money."

Nikki picked up an old cookie tin and shook it. Dead silence. "And our treasury is empty. I mean capital E–M–P–T–Y!"

It was summer vacation. The Apple Park Gang had gathered in their secret clubhouse, an old abandoned gazebo in Apple Park. Long ago, brass bands had entertained people in the gazebo. Then a new bandshell was built, and everybody forgot about the old building. Ben, Nikki, and Davey had discovered the round, vine-covered gazebo at the beginning of the summer and decided it was a perfect place for a secret

clubhouse. Now the gang had to find a way to earn money for their club.

"C'mon, doesn't anybody have an idea?" Ben asked.

They all shook their heads glumly.

"I could loan the club some of my baby-sitting money," Nikki offered. She baby-sat a pair of six-year-old twins, Mike and Max Morrissey, when their mother was working. This week Mrs. Morrissey was taking a stay-at-home vacation to "catch up on things," so Nikki had a lot of free time.

"Thanks, Nikki," Ben said. "That's good to know in an emergency. But we'd better not start borrowing money. We should earn it instead."

The Apple Park Gang sank into silence. Carrie, the newest member of the gang, slipped a rock 'n' roll tape into her stereophonic, dual-cassette, four-speaker, graphic equalizer, high-velocity, screaming yellow boom box and turned the volume up high. Red lights flashed all along the front.

"I've got it!" Ben shouted over the music. He motioned to Carrie to turn the volume down. "We'll wash cars. We can bring buckets and sponges from home, and there's plenty of water in the lake—"

Davey interrupted. "Cars aren't allowed in the park."

"You're right, I forgot about that," Ben said.

He sighed. "Well, that's the only idea I've come up with. Looks like I'll never be able to buy more film."

Carrie turned the volume up again. She opened a bag of cookies and took one out. After she took a bite, she stopped. She flipped off the boom box.

"I know what we can do!" she shouted. "We can bake cookies and sell them in the park. We'll make a fortune!" Carrie looked at the rest of the gang expectantly.

"That's a great idea . . . except for one thing." Ben looked at each of his friends. "Who knows how to bake cookies?"

"Not me," Nikki said.

"Me, neither," Davey added. He looked at Carrie. "Do you?"

"Sure. Anybody knows that. You just mix up some flour and sugar and eggs and water and milk and . . ." She stopped. The rest of the gang stared at her, waiting for the next ingredient. Carrie blushed. "Okay. So I don't know how to make cookies. But I still think it's a good idea."

"I think it would be an even better idea if you passed the cookies around," Davey suggested, pointing to the paper bag next to Carrie.

Carrie, who was not always known for her generosity, hesitated a moment, then passed the bag of cookies to Davey. He took one and gave one to Nikki and Ben.

Everyone munched in silence. Pretty soon there was a loud knock on the gazebo door.

"Anyone in there?" called a familiar voice.

Ben jumped up and opened the door. "Hi, Mr. P. What are you doing here?"

Mr. P's real name was Spyros Papadopoulos. But no one could pronounce Spyros Papadopoulos, so they all called him Mr. P. He was the park keeper and the only adult who knew about the secret clubhouse.

"Oh, just making my rounds." Mr. P looked them all over. "Is something wrong? You kids don't look too happy today."

"We want to earn some money, but we haven't come up with any good ideas," Ben answered gloomily.

Mr. P grinned. "Well, isn't it lucky I stopped by!"

"Have you got an idea for us?" Ben asked eagerly.

"Well, with Apple Park Day coming up next Saturday. . ." Mr. P stopped in midsentence and raised his eyebrows mysteriously.

"Apple Park Day?" the gang asked in one voice. "What's Apple Park Day?"

Mr. P banged his palm lightly on his forehead. "Oh, didn't I tell you?" He pretended to be confused.

Davey jumped up and grabbed the park keeper's sleeve. "C'mon, Mr. P, stop teasing. What's Apple Park Day?"

"Tell us," Ben cried.

Nikki narrowed her eyes. "I bet this is another one of your jokes!" she said.

Mr. P burst out laughing. "No, this is no joke. And it would be a great way for you kids to make some money and help out Apple Park at the same time."

The park keeper explained that the Apple Park Council had been trying to think of ways to get more people to come to the park. The idea they had chosen was to hold a day-long party in the park. It would be called Apple Park Day, and it was scheduled for the following Saturday.

Ben wrinkled his brow. "It sounds like a great idea, but I don't see how a party in Apple Park will help us earn money."

Mr. P held up his hand. "Hold on, I'm just getting to that part. There'll be all kinds of things going on: contests, competitions, food, music. I figure you kids could set up a booth and sell something, or run a competition, or—"

"And we get to keep the money we make?" Nikki asked.

"You bet," Mr. P answered.

"Wow!" Nikki exclaimed. "Now all we have to do is figure out something to sell." She glanced at Carrie. "Besides cookies."

Carrie cocked her head to one side and stuck out her tongue.

"Well, I'd better be going," the park keeper

said, heading for the door. Then he noticed Ben's photographs on the wall. "Say, these are pretty good pictures. Who took 'em?"

"Me," Ben said. "Want me to take yours?"

"Sure would," said Mr. P, buttoning the top button on his shirt and adjusting his hat. "I've never had my picture taken in my park keeper's uniform."

Mr. P stood very still and straight while Ben pressed the shutter. Then he watched over Ben's shoulder as his picture slowly emerged on the shiny white paper.

"That's a great picture," said Mr. P. He held the photograph out in front of him. "In fact, I'd like to buy it." He reached into his pocket, pulled out a dollar bill, and handed it to Ben. "Is that enough?"

Ben pushed the money away. "You can have the picture, Mr. P." A big smile slowly spread across Ben's face. "You've just given me a great idea."

"For what?" Mr. P looked confused.

"For Apple Park Day. I'm going to take people's pictures!"

"And sell them?" Davey asked.

"Why not?" Ben said. "Mr. P wanted to buy his picture, didn't he?"

"And so will a lot of other people," the park keeper said. He slipped the photo in his shirt pocket and stepped out the door. Then he stopped and turned around. "By the way, some-one donated two boats to Apple Park. How would you kids like to fix them up for me? It'd be a big help, and I might even be able to pay you for your time."

"That sounds like fun," said Davey.

"It sounds gross," said Carrie. "I could break a nail."

Nikki rolled her eyes. "C'mon, Carrie," she said. "We owe Mr. P a favor. Besides, the trea-sury could use the money."

Carrie frowned. "Oh, all right! I guess I can change into work clothes."

"Thanks, kids. I appreciate the help," said Mr. P. "Meanwhile, do you think you can get those boats painted in time for the party?"

Ben stood in the doorway. "Sure thing. Two shiny new boats coming right up." He waved to Mr. P, then called, "By the way, if it's okay with you, we may stay late in the park this week working on our projects for Apple Park Day."

"It's okay with me," the park keeper called back.

All afternoon and into the evening, the Apple Park Gang tried to think of what to do to earn money for Apple Park Day. Except for Ben's idea to take pictures, no one could think of a thing.

"I'd better get some practice with the few shots I have left," Ben said. He looked out the gazebo window. "It's getting dark. Let's head up Apple Hill. I'll take a picture of the park in the moonlight."

"How can you take pictures at night?" Nikki asked. "You don't have a flash."

"No, but I have this," Ben answered. He pulled a short, thin cable with a plunger at one end out of his pocket.

Davey examined the device closely, then shook his head. "I give up. What is it?"

"It's a cable release. I put the camera on a chair or a table so it can't move. Then I attach the cable, and then I push the plunger. As long as I hold it down, the shutter stays open. If I hold it down long enough, I can take pictures with hardly any light at all."

The lights of the park cast shadows along the walking path as Ben and his friends made their way toward Apple Hill. A light breeze rustled the leaves high in the trees. The moon disappeared for a few seconds behind an elephant-shaped cloud.

Carrie shuddered. "Oooh, it's spooky out here. I think you should be a daytime photographer, Ben."

"Anyone can be a daytime photographer," Ben answered dramatically. "Moonlight pictures will be my specialty."

As they passed the petting zoo, the gang could hear the soft bellow of a calf waiting for its

supper, then the baaing of a lamb. They were about to turn onto the winding path that led to the top of Apple Hill when Ben, who was in the lead, suddenly stopped.

"Ooopf," Nikki muttered, bumping into him. "Don't stop so— "

Ben touched his index finger to his lips. His eyes darted from side to side. "Did you hear that?"

"I heard the sheep," Davey answered. "Why are you whispering?"

"*Shhh!* Listen!"

Everybody listened. Pitiful, who had been asleep in Davey's arms, perked up one ear. He made a low, rumbling growl, then went back to sleep.

In the distance, the calf bellowed softly again. Then came another sound.

This one was a creepy sound. It came in waves, first soft, then louder, then soft again. And it was getting closer by the second!

CHAPTER
TWO

"**I** think it's moving toward us!" Nikki said.

"Let's get out of here!" Carrie whispered.

"Not until we find out where it's coming from," Ben said.

"Ben's right," Davey agreed. "Besides, this is exciting!"

Walking carefully but quickly along the path, the gang made its way toward the sound.

Another cloud glided silently past the moon.

Carrie started to whimper. Nikki grabbed her arm. "Don't be a scaredy-cat!" she hissed.

"There's nothing to be afraid of," Ben said bravely. "It's just a sound. Sounds can't hurt you." He was acting brave, but Ben was glad the rest of the gang couldn't see how scared he was. There were shivers running up and down his back.

"Yeow!" yelled Carrie. "Something's grabbing me!" She swatted the air around her bare legs.

"It's just the bushes," Ben cried. "Hurry up!"

"They feel more like claws! I don't like it out here in the dark. I wish I was home," Carrie moaned.

With Ben in front, the gang groped its way along the rough trail, heading in the direction of the mysterious noise. The nearer they got, the louder it grew. It started to sound a lot like music, too.

"I think it's someone singing," Davey said. "Someone with an old, creaky voice."

"That's ridiculous!" Nikki exclaimed. "Who'd be singing in the park—at night—in the moonlight?"

"A . . . a g-g-ghost?" Carrie's voice quivered.

"There's no such thing as ghosts," Nikki quickly replied.

"Oh, yeah? Well, I've heard stories about ghosts—" Carrie snapped.

"*Shhh!*" Ben hissed. With one hand cupped behind his ear, he tilted his head and listened. The rest of the gang listened, too.

Then a grin slowly spread across Ben's face. He slapped his thigh and started to laugh. "I know what it is! It's the carousel! It's music from the carousel! Can you believe we let ourselves get spooked by carousel music?"

Carrie looked doubtful. "I never heard of the carousel running in the dark." She paused. "But if it *is* the carousel, that means there's someone there . . . and maybe that someone doesn't want company!" She gnawed nervously on her fingernail.

Davey didn't laugh, either. He looked at Ben and shook his head. "It can't be the carousel. No one rides it at night."

"Or hardly ever in the day, either," Nikki added. "It's too old, and some of the horses are broken."

Ben answered, "Broken or not, I still say it's the carousel. But there's only one way to find out." He started off again in the direction of the sound.

"Do we have to find out *now*?" Carrie called in a trembling voice. "Can't we come back during the day?"

Ben stopped. He looked impatient. "What's the point of coming back during the day when we want to find out why it's running at night?"

"So it won't be so s-s-scary?"

"Aw, c'mon." Ben motioned for Carrie and the rest to follow him.

With the three scrambling behind, Ben dashed off in the direction of the sound.

Soon he spotted an opening in the bushes ahead, and beyond it he caught a glimpse of the carousel. Ben couldn't tell if it was moving, but he could hear the music louder now. He stopped and waited for the others to catch up.

"See? I told you. It's just the—" But before Ben could finish his sentence, the music stopped!

Nikki shivered. "Why do you suppose it stopped? Do you think they saw us or heard us coming?"

"Who?" Davey asked.

"Whoever turned off the music."

"How do you know *anyone* turned it off?" Ben asked.

"Well, somebody turned it off!" Carrie whispered through clenched teeth. "A minute ago there was music. Now it's stopped. That means *somebody* turned it off!" She gnawed another fingernail. "I don't like this. Let's get out of here right now!"

"Maybe Carrie's right," Davey said. "Maybe someone's there who doesn't want company. *Our* company. Maybe we should leave."

"Not until I've taken a picture," Ben said. "If there *is* someone lurking around the carousel, maybe it'll show up in the picture. I've got to find out." Before anyone could stop him, Ben started for an opening in the bushes.

"C'mon. We'd better stick close to him," Nikki whispered, "in case he needs help."

"I don't like this one bit," Carrie muttered.

Ben tiptoed through the opening. In the distance, the carousel horses stood silently, one behind the other, beneath the striped canopy. "I can't get a good shot from here," he whispered. "I'm going closer."

"No! Don't!" Carrie grabbed at Ben's shirttail.

"What are you so nervous about? An empty carousel isn't dangerous," Ben said. "Wait here. I'll be right back."

Ben stepped into the bright moonlight. Everything was still except for the sound of his sneaker cracking a dry twig. He crept toward the circle of prancing horses. When he was close enough that the carousel filled the camera frame, he knelt down and set the camera on a rock. *I don't want the camera to shake or the picture will be blurry,* he thought. He pressed the plunger on the end of the remote cable, counted slowly to ten, and released it. With a small click, the camera went off.

Ben grabbed the camera and quickly crept back through the opening in the bushes. He held up the shiny white square of photographic paper. "Got it! It's too dark to see what it looks like tonight. Let's meet at the clubhouse early tomorrow morning. I'll bring my picture of the . . ." He leaned toward Carrie and laughed a devilish laugh. ". . . *the haunted carousel!*"

Mrs. Ferber was watching a TV movie when Ben got back from Apple Park. His father

was sitting at the kitchen table reading the newspaper.

"Hi, Dad," Ben said. He slid the camera strap over his head and gently set the camera on the table. Next to it he put the picture of the carousel.

Ben's father picked up the photograph. "Moonlight photography, huh? Isn't that the carousel in the park?"

"Yes. I just took it. I wanted to prove . . ." Ben decided not to tell his father about the strange goings-on at the carousel, at least not until he'd had time to study the photograph himself. "I wanted to prove . . . uh . . . that I could take pictures by moonlight."

"Well, let's have a look," Mr. Ferber said, leaning back in his chair. "I think it's a darn good picture. I like the moonlight shining on the horses, and I like the strange shapes of the shadows, too." He held the photo up closer to his face and squinted. Then he chuckled. "Is that one of your friends hiding in the bushes?"

"What?" Ben gasped, grabbing the picture. He looked closely at the photo. "Where, Dad? Where do you see someone?"

Mr. Ferber smiled and gently took the photo from his son. "It's a little hard to see, but right there, in the bushes." He pointed to a clump of shrubbery behind the carousel. "I'm sure it's a person." He looked up at Ben. "Now, who would it be if it isn't one of your friends?" He chuckled and nudged Ben with his elbow. "A ghost, maybe?"

Ben studied the photo. What he saw made his heart skip a beat. His father was right! A mysterious figure was crouching, half-hidden, in the bushes.

How could he have missed it when he was taking the photo? How could Nikki, Davey, and Carrie have missed it, too? Was the figure watching them the whole time?

Ben put the photo on the table. A chill prickled up and down his spine.

"What's the matter, son?" Mr. Ferber asked. "You look like you've just seen a ghost. . . ."

A thick fog hung over Apple Park as Ben made his way to the gazebo early the next morning. Nikki, Davey, and Carrie were already there when he arrived. "Whew! That's some fog!" he exclaimed. "It's like the middle of the night out there!"

"It was so thick I could hardly find the clubhouse," Nikki said. "Good thing I had my compass." She pulled a small black case out of her pocket.

"Nikki Ferris, the gadget freak!" Davey said. "What *is* that thing?"

Nikki smiled proudly and held up the gadget for her friends to see. "It's a pocket calculator and a compass and a watch and an alarm clock and a stopwatch and a—" she pressed a button on the side, "—a retractable magnifying glass."

"Magnifying glass?" Ben asked.

Nikki nodded. "It magnifies four times the original size."

Ben snapped his fingers. "That's just what we need!" He pulled the photograph of the carousel from his shirt pocket. "We may have a ghost on our hands! Here, take a look." Ben held up the photograph.

Nikki, Davey, and Carrie gathered around him.

"I see a carousel, and some bushes," said Davey. "So what?"

"I see some dark shadows," Carrie said.

"I certainly don't see any ghosts," Nikki added impatiently.

"Look again," Ben said, "and this time, use your magnifying glass."

Nikki held the glass close to the picture. She moved it slowly over the shiny surface. "Horse . . . horse . . . another horse . . . bush . . . bush . . ." Suddenly she stopped mumbling. She held the glass steadily over one spot in the picture. "Person!" she gasped.

Davey grabbed the photo. "Let me see!" Holding the glass over the same spot, he whistled softly.

"See? I was right," Carrie cried. "There *was* a ghost. It was watching us all the time. It grabbed my legs. It—"

Nikki stamped her foot. "There's no such thing as ghosts! And even if there was, you couldn't take their picture because you can see right through them." She pointed to the figure in the photo. "That's a real person, not a ghost."

Carrie shuddered. "I don't know which is worse. . . ."

"It's a person, all right," Ben said. "Dad spotted it last night. He thought it was one of us." He stroked his chin. "The question is, who is it, and why was he hiding in the bushes behind the carousel after dark? And is he the one who turned the music off?" He narrowed his eyes and nodded his head solemnly. "There's something funny going on here, and I'm going to find out what it is."

Nikki fiddled with her magnifying glass. "What do you think we should do?"

"Go back to the carousel and take more pictures," Ben said as he crossed to the window and looked out. "It's still pretty foggy, perfect for ghosts to sneak around in." He paused and muttered, "Or for someone *real* to sneak around in . . ." He started for the door. "Anyone coming with me?"

"Are you crazy?" Carrie yelled. "With all those weirdo things going on, you want to go back to the carousel? You couldn't pay me to go back there." Carrie folded her arms across her chest and stuck out her chin.

Davey and Nikki looked at each other. Finally, Nikki shrugged and took a step toward Ben. "I'll come," she said. "There's safety in numbers."

"Me, too," Davey said. "I'll bring Pitiful. He'll be able to pick up any strange scents."

"How can a senseless dog pick up scents?" Carrie sneered.

Ben, who was already halfway out the door, turned and said, "Well, Carrie, are you coming or not?"

Carrie dug her hands in her pockets and paced back and forth silently. "I'm not staying here alone, that's for sure," she said finally.

The gang had just passed the petting zoo and were turning the corner by the bandshell when, out of the fog, came the sound—the same ghostly musical sound they had heard the night before!

"Hurry up! We've got to get there before it stops!" Ben yelled.

Ben's camera thumped against his chest as he ducked and dodged branches on the winding path. *I wish it wasn't so foggy*, he thought. *If there is someone on the carousel, I won't be able to get a clear picture.*

His heart pounded, and he found himself getting a little scared, but Ben didn't slow down.

When the gang was almost at the carousel, the music suddenly stopped.

"Oh, no!" Ben cried.

"Someone turned it off again," Nikki whispered.

Carrie shivered. "What if it's the same some-one who was in the bushes last night?"

"He might still be there," Davey said.

"If the fog lifts, I'll take a picture," Ben said. He started tiptoeing toward the carousel. "Maybe we'll find another mystery figure lurking in the background."

Pitiful wriggled in Davey's arms. "Be careful," Davey warned. "Pitiful is acting a little weird. Maybe he sees someone we can't see."

As Ben neared the carousel, a breeze came up and the fog lifted. Not wasting a moment, Ben pressed the camera's viewfinder against his eye and snapped the shutter.

Then, as quickly as it had lifted, the fog set-tled back down, blanketing the carousel and the kids in a soft cloud of gray.

Ben tore off the undeveloped photograph from the front of the camera. "We'll check this out under your magnifying glass when we get back to the clubhouse," he said to Nikki.

By the time the gang arrived back at the ga-zebo, the morning sun had burned off the fog, exposing a bright blue, cloudless sky.

Ben carefully laid his camera in a corner and flopped down on the clubhouse floor. "Boy, I can't wait to study this picture," he said excitedly.

Nikki handed her magnifying glass to Ben. He took the glass and the photo over to the window, where the light was streaming in.

"Personally, I don't want to see the picture," Carrie said to Ben. She sat down cross-legged on the floor. Davey and Nikki sat beside her. "It's a beautiful day, and I'd rather think about something else besides creepy carousels, ghostly music, and mysterious people lurking in bushes."

"Me, too," Nikki said, "but who can think about anything else?"

"What about Apple Park Day?"

"That's a good idea," Nikki said. "I wish I knew what I was going to do to earn some money."

"I haven't thought of anything, either," Davey said glumly.

"I decided last night what I'm going to do," Carrie said smugly.

"What?" Nikki and Ben asked in one voice.

"I'm going to paint faces. I have a whole set of greasepaints that my aunt gave me last year, and my mother has dozens of old lipsticks. She already said I could use them. I'm going to call my booth 'Carrie's Creations.' I'm—"

"Holy cow!" Ben yelled. He was standing in the light of the window, holding the photograph.

"I *knew* we'd end up talking about that picture," Carrie muttered.

"Holy cow!" Ben repeated, gazing at the photo.

Nikki and Davey scrambled to their feet.

"What is it?" asked Davey.

"Another mysterious figure?" Nikki asked.

Ben held out the photograph. "See for your-self!" he cried. "Just see for yourself!"

CHAPTER
THREE

Nikki squinted at the photograph. "I don't see anything," she said.

Davey looked confused. "Me, neither."

"That's just it," Ben said. "It's not what you see. It's what you *don't* see."

"That's ridiculous," Carrie muttered, rolling her eyes. She sat cross-legged on the floor watching her three friends. "How can you see what you don't see?"

Ben ignored Carrie and handed Nikki the magnifying glass. "Take another look."

Moving the glass slowly over the shiny surface, Nikki again studied the picture. Davey looked over her shoulder. "It was pretty foggy when you took this, and it's hard to see . . ." she began. Then she paused. "Wait a minute!" She looked at Ben and nodded. "Yes . . . I think I do see what you don't see."

Carrie flopped backward on the floor. "Aaargh! First you see what you see! Then you see what you don't see! I can't stand it!"

"It's missing, isn't it? One of the carousel horses is missing!" Ben exclaimed.

"It sure is!" Nikki agreed.

"You can see it clearly under the magnifying glass," Davey added, taking the photograph from Nikki. "I mean, you can see that it's not there."

Carrie sat back up. This time she looked serious. "Really?" she asked. "Is a horse really missing?"

Nikki held out the photograph. "See for yourself."

"But that's ridiculous!" Carrie exclaimed after staring at the picture. "Who'd want an old broken-down, no-tail, maneless carousel horse?"

Ben shrugged. "Who knows? Maybe there's something about those carousel horses that we don't know." He narrowed his eyes and lowered his voice. "But one thing I know for sure—I'm going to find out right now!"

Carrie groaned, "Oh, no! Not again!"

"What's the matter? You're not scared to go to the carousel in broad daylight, are you?" Davey asked.

Carrie looked sheepish. "I'm not scared. It gives me the creeps, that's all . . . people hiding in the bushes, horses disappearing—it's creepy!" She shuddered. "Besides, we should be working on those boats for Mr. P. We did promise, you know."

"I guess you're right," Ben said. "Tell you what. We'll take a quick detour around by the carousel, then we'll go to the boathouse. Deal?"

"Deal," Nikki and Davey said together.

"Guess I'm outvoted," Carrie sighed, standing up and brushing off the seat of her designer shorts.

Carrie picked up her screaming yellow boom box, Davey picked up Pitiful, Nikki popped her calculator–compass–watch–alarm clock–magnifying glass into her pocket, and the three followed Ben out the gazebo door.

By cutting across the footbridge and snaking through the overgrown trail that connected to the bike path, the Apple Park Gang made it to the carousel in no time.

"Look! It's back!" Davey called out. "The missing horse is back! And it looks brand-new!"

Ben lowered his camera and looked closely at the carousel. Davey was right! All the horses were there.

"What's Wheels doing here?" Nikki asked.

Sitting on a horse with a missing tail and a broken hoof was Wheels Gilligan, the bully of

Appleby Corners. Next to him was the shiny new horse.

"I don't know, but I say we find out." Ben led the rest of the gang over to where Wheels was sitting.

"Hello, Wheels," Ben said. "What's a tough guy like you doing riding a carousel?"

Carrie smirked and Nikki elbowed her.

"For your information, Ferber," Wheels sneered, ignoring Carrie, "I was riding my bike, and I stopped to take a rest."

Ben hopped up onto the carousel and stroked the shiny, newly painted horse next to Wheels. "Looks like someone's fixed up this old horse. Any idea who?"

Wheels shrugged. "Nope."

"What have you been painting?" Nikki asked Wheels.

Wheels's face flushed and his eyes darted from Ben to Nikki. "Nothing."

"There's paint all over your shirt and hands. I figure that means you've been painting."

Wheels rubbed the paint from his fingers onto his shirt and tucked his hands between his legs.

"Hey," he said to Ben. "Where'd you get that camera?"

"My dad," Ben answered.

"Wanna take my picture?" Wheels leered.

"Might break the lens," Carrie mumbled.

"Sure, I'll take your picture," Ben said, "but

not on that old broken-down horse. How about standing next to this shiny new one?"

Wheels hopped down. He leaned against the new horse and grinned a big, cheesy grin.

Ben pressed the shutter. With a click and a whir, the photograph slid out of the camera.

"Let me see it!" Wheels grabbed for the undeveloped picture.

"Don't touch it!" Ben shouted. "I'll show it to you when it's done."

"Can we see, too?"

Ben looked over his shoulder. Standing next to him were Mike and Max Morrissey, the six-year-old twins Nikki baby-sat. The twins had found out about the kids' clubhouse, but Nikki swore them to secrecy by promising to let them join the gang when they were in the second grade.

"Hi, guys," Nikki said, smiling. "What are you doing here?"

"We were sitting on the carousel . . ." began Mike.

Max finished Mike's sentence. ". . . until Wheels told us we couldn't."

"Wheels told you you couldn't sit on the carousel?" Ben repeated. "Why?"

This time Max spoke first. "He said it wasn't safe."

"That's funny," Davey said, scratching his head. He turned to Wheels. "Who told you it wasn't safe?"

Wheels looked down at his feet and mumbled.

"What did you say, Wheels?" Ben asked.

"I said it's none of your business," Wheels snapped.

Ben turned to the twins. "Don't worry, guys. We'll work it out. You'll be able to hang out here again."

A look of relief passed over the twins' faces. "Thanks, Ben," Mike said. "We have to go home now." The twins waved and walked off together.

" 'Bye, guys," Nikki yelled after them. "I'll baby-sit you again when your mom goes back to work."

Ben jumped down from the carousel. "We'd better be going if we want to get those boats painted."

"Hey, what about my picture?" Wheels yelled.

Ben stopped. "Oh, I almost forgot." He held up the photograph for Wheels to see.

Wheels leaned down from the carousel. "Pretty good," he mumbled. "Can I have it?"

"Sorry," Ben answered. "I'm keeping all the photographs I take in the park. I'm uh . . . I'm going to make a book out of them," he added hastily.

"You are?" Nikki asked, surprised.

Ben turned his head and winked. "You remember . . . the book . . . the park book?"

Nikki, Davey, and Carrie all caught Ben's signal.

"Oh, yes, uh . . . I remember now. You did mention it," Nikki said, hiding her confusion.

Ben grabbed Carrie's shirttail and motioned to his friends. "C'mon. Let's go. We've got some boats to fix up."

The gang quickly hurried away from the carousel, leaving Wheels with his mouth hanging open. As soon as they were out of hearing distance, Nikki turned to Ben. "What's this about a book on the park?" she asked.

Ben stopped and pulled out the photograph. "I was glad Wheels asked me to take this picture because I'd noticed something suspicious, and I wanted to get some proof."

Davey frowned. "Proof of what?"

Ben pointed to the photograph as he spoke. "Look at the color of the new horse. Now look at the color of the paint on Wheels's shirt and hands."

"It's the same!" Carrie cried.

Ben nodded. "Right! I'll bet you anything Wheels Gilligan has something to do with the missing horse. I don't know what, but this photograph may help us find out." He tapped the corner of the picture. "That's why I didn't want to give it to him."

Davey laughed. "So the book is just something you made up to throw Wheels off the track?"

Ben winked and tucked the photograph back into his shirt pocket. "Righto!"

Nikki pulled out her new gadget and checked the time. "If we want to work on those boats today, we'd better get started. It's really late."

Ben nodded. "We can find out what Wheels is up to soon enough. Let's get going."

The gang found the two rowboats resting upside down on sawhorses in the boathouse. They were in pretty bad shape, just like Mr. P had said. Their paint was peeling, and they had holes in their bottoms big enough to squint through.

On a bench along the back wall of the boathouse was a lineup of materials: paint scrapers, sandpaper, caulking, cans of paint and brushes—and directions from Mr. P.

"Well, let's get started," Ben said. He handed out the paint scrapers. "Two on a boat."

"This looks like a horrible job," Carrie said with a grimace. "But hopefully some music will make it go faster." She set her screaming yellow boom box on the bench next to the paintbrushes and slipped a tape of her favorite group, Designer Genes, into the slot. She turned the volume up high.

Davey set Pitiful, who was asleep as usual, down on the floor. At the sound of the music, Pitiful opened his eyes and looked around. Then he curled up and went back to sleep.

For the next half hour, the four scraped and sanded the old boats. Carrie's music filled the boathouse. When both sides of the first tape had played, she said, "Anybody want to hear 'Elvis Presley's Greatest Hits'? It's the only other tape I brought."

"If we have to," Nikki groaned. "He's my least favorite singer."

Carrie shrugged and slipped the tape into the tape deck. She pressed the play button. Elvis Presley started crooning, "Hound Dog."

Suddenly, and without warning, Pitiful's ears underwent a remarkable change. They shot straight up, from their usual full droop, toward the ceiling. His eyes opened, and his whole body began to twitch.

All four of the Apple Park Gang dropped their scrapers and their jaws at the same time. Pitiful jerked his muzzle, then his head, then his whole body, and flipped over onto his back. Then he stretched his four legs straight up into the air and started to howl.

When the song was over, Pitiful flopped onto his stomach, tucked his four short legs under his body, and went back to sleep.

Davey and his friends stared in amazement at the basset hound. Davey's face lit up. He snapped his fingers. "That's it!" he yelled. "That's what I'll do!"

Everyone looked mystified.

Davey held his hands above his head and gazed toward the ceiling. "I can see it all now. The world's one and only singing dog."

"What *are* you talking about?" Carrie asked.

Davey dropped his hands. "Don't you see? Pitiful will be my booth for Apple Park Day. I'll charge admission to hear 'The One and Only Singing Dog'!" He turned to Carrie. "But I'll have to borrow your Elvis tape."

"You can borrow the tape, but I can't imagine anyone in their right mind *paying* to hear that . . . that *animal* howl."

"I'll admit it's a little weird." Davey knelt down and patted the sleeping dog. "But I have faith in you, ol' boy," he murmured. "As long as I can keep you awake," he added.

After another hour of sanding and scraping, the Apple Park Gang finally put down their scrapers and sandpaper and called it a day. The sun was setting and they were all exhausted.

"There's still lots to do," Nikki said. "Let's meet here tomorrow morning and work all day on the boats."

As the gang left the boathouse and headed toward the park entrance, Ben stopped short. "Looks like another good night to practice my moonlight photography. Pretty soon I'll be a pro!"

"Stay away from that creepy carousel," Carrie warned.

"Don't worry," Ben said. "I'm heading for Apple Hill, not the carousel."

Except for the faraway whine of traffic, the

park was still as Ben ambled along the bike path that twisted and turned through the trees. He whistled "Hound Dog" softly. His camera bounced gently against his chest. *I really like taking pictures,* he thought. *Once I earn some money, I'll be able to—*

Then Ben stopped still in his tracks. He stopped whistling. He listened carefully. There it was again! That sound! That ghostly musical sound!

CHAPTER
FOUR

Not even Ben's booming heart could drown out the ghostly sound. He swallowed hard and stood as though cemented to the spot. He felt as if each of his feet weighed a hundred pounds.

Then he took a deep breath and let it out slowly. "Calm down, Ferber," he told himself. "It's just music. It's just carousel music . . . kids' stuff. Nothing to be nervous about."

With his heart still thumping madly, Ben scrambled along the bike path that wound through the park. As he neared the carousel, the music grew louder.

Just ahead, Ben could make out an opening in

the bushes. Right beyond the opening, the carousel played. On tiptoes, he crept to the opening and peered through.

There, in the moonlight, stood the carousel. Up and down and around and around, the painted horses galloped in perfect time to the music.

"So far, so good," Ben said to himself. His heart was still thumping in his chest as he slipped through bushes toward the circling horses. Ben set the camera on a tree stump, framed the shot in the viewfinder, and had almost pressed the plunger on the remote cable. Then something in the viewfinder caught his attention.

"Holy cow!" he whispered. "What's that?"

There, by the light of the moon, he saw a ghostly figure . . . riding the carousel!

Ben stood absolutely still. He blinked. He squinted at the figure on the horse. Was he seeing things? He blinked again. There was no doubt about it—he wasn't seeing things.

"If I don't get a picture of this, everyone will think I made it up," Ben muttered. "Especially Nikki."

Ben dropped to his knees and started crawling quietly toward a large boulder about twenty feet from the carousel. "I've *got* to get a picture," he muttered. "This may be my only chance."

With his knees still knocking, he set the camera on the stone, pressed the plunger on the

remote cable, counted to ten, then released it. He took a deep breath as the camera went off. It sounded so loud. What if the ghostly figure heard it? Luckily, the music from the carousel covered up the noise from the camera.

I'd better take another picture in case the first one doesn't come out, Ben thought. He pressed the plunger again. But this time nothing happened. He gently shook the camera and pressed again. Nothing.

Ben sat on the ground and thought. There was no reason for the camera to break now. Maybe he was doing something wrong. Or . . . or . . . *How stupid can I get?* he thought. *I've run out of film!*

As he fiddled with the camera, Ben suddenly realized the music had stopped. He looked toward the carousel. The rider had disappeared!

"Wow," Ben muttered softly, staring at the spot where the rider had been. "There's something really strange going on here." He picked up his camera and shook his head. It was getting late and his parents were probably wondering where he was. The mystery of the creepy carousel would have to wait one more day.

Ben could hear his father hammering in the basement when he bounded up the front steps and into the kitchen. "Mom, Dad—I'm home!"

"Okay, son," he heard his father call. "Your

mother left a meat loaf sandwich and milk for you in the refrigerator."

Ben grabbed the sandwich and headed for the study, where there were two of the biggest, heaviest books Ben had ever lifted. They were Volumes I and II of the *Oxford English Dictionary*. "There's no word in the English language you can't find in the OED," Ben's father had told him.

Ben had been skeptical. "How can you fit all those words in just two books?"

Mr. Ferber had laughed. "Print small and use this." He'd held up a rectangular magnifying glass that was nearly as big as a post card.

Ben went straight to the OED. He pulled the magnifying glass out of a little drawer above the books and held it over the photograph. "Oh, no," he groaned. "I forgot about the movement!"

Instead of the clear picture Ben had imagined, the photo of the carousel was blurry with motion. The stripes on the canopy had run together. The horses were followed by outlines which showed every time they had gone up and down. And there was no sign of the mysterious figure.

"Where is he?" Ben mumbled. "He's got to be here. I *know* I saw him." He raised the glass higher above the patterned surface so that it magnified even more.

To get a better look, Ben crossed the room

and studied the photograph under the reading lamp. "It was pretty dark, but I know—" All at once he stopped muttering and tilted the picture toward the light. "There he is! I knew it! I *knew* I wasn't seeing things! He's a . . . He's a . . . *She!*"

Under the powerful magnification of the glass, Ben was positive he was looking at a woman, but because of the blur he couldn't tell if she was young or old, a stranger or someone he knew. The ghost rider wore a big black hat pulled down low over her head. A filmy scarf covered her face. She seemed to be wearing a long skirt, and a cape hung from her shoulders.

When he looked again at the picture, Ben saw something that made him catch his breath. "Wow!" he cried. "Another carousel horse is missing!"

Ben whistled through his teeth. There was something very strange going on at the carousel. One minute music was playing. The next, it stopped. One minute there was a rider, then he—that is, *she*—disappeared. Carousel horses came and went from one day to another. What was going on?

"What's wrong, Ben?" Ben's thoughts were interrupted by his father's voice in the study doorway. Mr. Ferber came over to where Ben was standing. "What have we got here? Another ghostly picture of the carousel?"

Ben nodded.

"It's kind of dark," Mr. Ferber said, "but I like the way you caught the movement. Very artistic. Can I take a look at it under the glass?"

Ben nodded and handed his father the magnifying glass.

"Hmmm," said Mr. Ferber, moving the glass up and down above the picture. "Very interesting." He studied it carefully, then said, "I see someone in a big black hat with a long flowing scarf sitting on a horse." He looked at Ben. "Is it one of your friends?"

Ben shrugged. "Uh . . . yeah, I guess so."

"Hmmm," repeated his father. "I see two more of your friends hiding in the bushes. One looks like he has a moustache. Were you guys having some kind of midnight costume party?"

Ben felt the color drain from his cheeks. "Did . . . did you say you saw two other people hiding in the bushes?" He took the photo and the magnifying glass from his father.

Mr. Ferber pointed to the picture. "Right there." He laughed. "Where did you kids get those dress-up clothes?"

Ben didn't answer. He held the glass over the spot where his father had pointed. There were two figures, all right. One was tall, with a moustache, the other was shorter, about Ben's size. The taller one was holding something the size of a large dog in his arms.

Mr. Ferber ruffled his son's hair. "I'm glad you and your friends are having such fun in Apple Park. Maybe after the park party, more people will start to enjoy it, too. Oh, by the way, Mr. P tells me you're going to take people's pictures on Apple Park Day."

"I guess so," Ben mumbled, staring at the picture. "If I can get some money to buy film."

Mr. Ferber laughed. "Tell you what, I'll loan you the money. But remember, it's a loan. That means you have to pay it back."

Ben grinned. "Thanks, Dad." Ben dashed out of the study and up the stairs to his bedroom. He closed the door, picked up the telephone, and called Nikki.

"Hello?" Nikki answered.

"Wait'll you hear what happened! You'll never believe it!" Between gasps for breath, Ben told her about what he had seen in the park and what he and his father had discovered in the photograph.

"I don't like the sound of this one little bit," Nikki said. "I think we should tell someone."

"Like who?"

"Like the police."

"They won't believe us. They'll think we're just a bunch of silly kids telling ghost stories."

There was silence on Nikki's end of the phone. Then she said, "Wait a minute, what about the picture?"

Ben asked, "What do you mean?"

"We could show them the picture, and then they'd believe us."

"Yeah, you're right—no, you're not."

"Why not?"

"Because I showed the picture to my dad, and he thought it was just us kids dressed up in funny costumes. The police might think the same thing." He paused. "But maybe you're right. Maybe we should tell someone."

There was more silence while Ben and Nikki both thought about whom to tell. "I know!" Nikki said excitedly. "Julia Forbes! She could talk about it on her show!"

Julia Forbes was an investigative reporter on the WAPG television evening news.

Ben didn't think telling Julia Forbes was a good idea. "We don't have enough proof yet to make a news story. All we've got are a couple of dark, foggy photographs. We need more evidence. And there's only one way to get it."

"You mean, go back to the carousel?"

"Right."

"Wait 'til Carrie hears about this!" Nikki said. "Going back to the carousel for more evidence will really give her the creeps." Nikki paused, then asked in a trembling voice, "Do we *have* to go at night?"

"That's when the ghost rider appears and when the horses disappear," said Ben firmly. "I have to photograph the thief actually taking a horse. We need proof."

"I suppose you're right," said Nikki in a small voice, "but it's still a little scary." She sighed. "Well, I'll see you tomorrow morning at the boathouse. Then we'll tell Carrie and Davey what's up."

Ben put down the phone and flopped onto his bed. He wondered if he was right in not telling Julia Forbes. Maybe he should have gone along with Nikki's idea to tell the police. Maybe the mystery rider was a big-time ghost—too big for the Apple Park Gang to handle.

"Nah," he said to himself. "There's nothing too big for the Apple Park Gang." He buried his face in his pillow. "I hope."

CHAPTER
FIVE

Davey, Nikki, and Carrie were hard at work painting the boats when Ben raced to the boathouse the next morning. As soon as he appeared in the doorway, Nikki dropped her brush and rushed up to him. "I've told Davey and Carrie about the picture. Let's see it, Ben! Let's see it!"

Ben pressed the photo to his chest and stepped backward. "Careful. Don't get paint marks on it. It's our only evidence so far."

Nikki wiped her hands on the bottom of her shirt. "I'm clean," she said, turning her hands palm up to show him. Ben handed her the picture. Out of her pocket she pulled the watch—

stopwatch–calculator–compass–alarm clock and pressed a button on the side. Out popped the little round magnifying glass.

"That's not strong enough," Ben said. "Use this." He held up his father's magnifying glass.

"Wow!" exclaimed Nikki. "You could see the hairs on a spider's leg with this!"

"Aaargh!" Carrie shuddered. "That's revolting."

Nikki, Carrie, and Davey studied the photograph.

"Do you see the two figures in the bushes?" Ben asked.

"Sure do," Nikki said. "And the ghost rider."

"And the missing horse," Davey added. He turned to Ben. "What do we do now?"

"We need more evidence—clear evidence— before we can go to the police." Ben thought for a moment. "We have to catch the thief in the act. That means I need to take more pictures—"

Nikki cut in. "But I thought you were nearly out of film."

"And *all* out of money," Carrie added.

"My dad loaned me some money," Ben said. "I'll buy film today. Let's meet at the entrance to the park tonight. Don't forget to tell your parents that Mr. P knows we're staying late in the park this week." He narrowed his eyes, rubbed his hands together, and laughed a sinister laugh. "Maybe we'll catch ourselves a horse thief!"

*   *   *

Later that night, stars twinkled in the sky. The moon shone clear and bright. Ben was the first to arrive at the Apple Park gate. His camera, loaded with fresh film, hung from his neck.

Nikki and Davey arrived next. Davey was carrying Pitiful, who, naturally, was asleep.

"How come you brought him?" Ben asked, pointing to the dog.

"Sometimes animals can see things humans can't," Davey explained. "I figure we're going to need all the eyes we can get tonight."

"I just hope he doesn't howl and give us away," Ben said. He looked around. "We're all here except Carrie. I bet she chickened out."

"I have not!" came a voice from the shadows. Out stepped a strange-looking figure. It was dressed entirely in black—a big floppy black hat, black gloves, a long black coat, and black boots.

"Carrie!" Ben, Nikki, and Davey yelled in one voice.

Ben poked his face under the brim of Carrie's hat. "Is that really you?"

"Of course it's me," Carrie snapped. "Who else would it be?"

"What on earth are you doing in that ridiculous outfit?" asked Nikki.

"Being sensible, that's what," Carrie said firmly. "Horse thieves and ghost riders can get very nasty." She waved one finger and raised her eyebrows knowingly. "But only if they can see you. And no one will be able to see me in this."

Ben looked Carrie up and down and slowly shook his head. "That's for sure! Look, we're not catching any thieves or ghosts by standing here. Let's go!"

Davey, Nikki, and a funny-looking Carrie followed closely behind Ben. When they reached the opening in the bushes, about thirty feet from the carousel, they stopped. All was quiet.

"Look," Davey said excitedly. He pointed to the carousel.

Sure enough, in the clear moonlight, it was easy to see that all the horses were there.

"They must have put it back after I left the park last night," Ben said. "Maybe that means they'll come back for another one tonight." He tapped the camera. "And this time I'm ready."

The Apple Park Gang sat on the ground and waited. No one said a word. Everyone listened.

Ten minutes passed. Then fifteen. Then twenty.

Carrie took off her hat and fanned her face. "Whew! I'm dying in these clothes. I think we've waited long enough. Let's go home."

"No!" Ben said sharply. "We've got to stay until the thief comes."

"Besides," Nikki added, "since I don't believe in ghosts, I want to meet this ghost rider in person!"

The gang sank back into silence.

Half an hour went by. "Pitiful is getting a little restless," Davey said eventually. "I hope he doesn't howl and give us away."

"Maybe he hears something. . . ." Ben stopped. His eyes darted from side to side. "What was that?" he whispered.

"I heard it, too," Nikki said. "I think it came from the carousel."

Huddled in the bushes, not daring to move a muscle, not even daring to blink, the gang watched. A ghostlike figure emerged out of the darkness and into the bright moonlight, wearing a big hat and a long, flowing scarf.

"She's getting onto the carousel!" Carrie cried under her breath.

"*Shhh!*" Ben whispered. "She might hear you!"

"Well, she won't *see* me," Carrie mumbled.

The figure climbed up onto the carousel, crossed between horses to the center, then pulled down a big lever. The music started. The horses began to slowly gallop up and down.

"I've got to take a picture of this," Ben said, crawling out of the bushes. "Wait here."

"Fine with me," Carrie said.

"Be careful," Davey whispered loudly.

"Don't let her see you," Nikki warned.

Ben crawled to the big stone about twenty feet from the carousel.

The figure climbed up onto a horse and was

riding around and around. She was also singing in the same creaky old voice Ben had heard before.

Ben set the camera on the stone and, using his remote cable, took a picture. The undeveloped picture shot out the front of the camera. He quickly tore it off. Then he snapped another one.

"There," he muttered. "If it's not too blurry, that should be more than enough evidence."

Ben was about to crawl back to his hiding place in the bushes when he spotted something moving in the shadows behind the carousel. His heart skipped a beat. Was it the thief—or thieves? Had someone seen him taking pictures?

He didn't know what to do. If he crawled back to the bushes now, the thief might see him. If he stayed where he was, so close to the carousel, he might also be seen. There was no telling what an angry horse thief would do!

Ben decided to stay put.

A tall man with a moustache stepped out into the moonlight. Ben wished he were close enough to see his face more clearly. The man ran along beside the carousel, then quickly jumped up onto the moving platform and pulled the lever. The horses stopped galloping. The moment the horses stopped, the ghost rider slid down from the horse and marched over to the man.

With the carousel now still, and his camera

sitting on the stone, Ben quickly pressed the plunger on the remote control. He counted to ten. Then he released the plunger. With a click and a whir, the photo came shooting out.

"Horse thief!" shrieked the ghost rider, hitting the man with what looked to Ben like an umbrella. "Horse thief!"

"Get out of here," yelled the man. "Go home where you belong before you get hurt."

Ben took another picture.

The ghost rider jumped off the carousel and disappeared into the night.

Though his heart was beating wildly, Ben sat as still as a statue. *What's going to happen next?* he wondered.

He didn't have long to wait.

Checking first to see that no one was watching, the man with the moustache slipped a large wrench from his back pocket and unscrewed one of the old, broken-down carousel horses. He lifted it off and set it by his feet.

"Holy cow!" Ben muttered. "The thief in action!" He snapped another shot.

Then, with two fingers between his lips, the man gave a short, sharp whistle. Out of the shadows emerged another, smaller figure who was carrying a large object.

Ben squinted, trying to make out what the object was. As the figure got closer, Ben sud-

denly realized exactly what it was. It was a carousel horse—a shiny new carousel horse!

As Ben snapped pictures, the tall man took the new horse and screwed it onto the carousel, where the old one had galloped just minutes before. Then, picking up the old horse, he and the shorter figure disappeared into the deepening shadows.

Picking up the undeveloped photographs, Ben crept back through the opening in the bushes. "Did you see that?" he cried. He held up the pictures. "I've got it all here! Proof! Evidence!"

"I saw it all, but I couldn't tell who they were," Nikki said excitedly.

"Me, neither," Davey agreed. "But," he added, "there was something very familiar about the short one. I think I've seen him before. Even Pitiful made funny noises when he came out of the shadows."

"I thought he looked familiar, too," Carrie said, biting on a fingernail.

Ben tapped on the photographs. "At least we've got some evidence now. C'mon. Let's go back to my house and see who we've caught!"

Back at Ben's house, the Apple Park Gang ran into Mr. Ferber's study. Ben pulled out the little drawer above the two volumes of the *Oxford English Dictionary* and took out the magnifying glass. He laid the photographs on the table under the lamp. Then, holding the glass just above the shiny surfaces, he slowly moved from one photograph to the other. As he moved, he let out a series of little gasps.

"What is it? What do you see?" Nikki asked.

"Holy cow!" Ben exclaimed.

"What!" Davey cried. "Tell us!"

"Wow!"

"Let me look, Ben." It was Carrie. She pushed Nikki and Davey aside to get a better look over Ben's shoulder.

Ben looked up from the photographs. His face was white, as though he'd just seen a ghost. "You're not going to believe what . . . no, *who* you see." He handed the glass to Carrie.

Carrie leaned over the table. She slowly moved the magnifying glass along the row of photographs. "This is serious!"

"What are we going to do?" Nikki asked when everyone had taken a good look at the pictures.

"I've already decided," said Ben. "It's time for us to call Julia Forbes!"

CHAPTER
SIX

"Julia Forbes will see you now," said the receptionist at WAPG. "Come with me." She turned and started down a long, red-carpeted hall.

The Apple Park Gang scrambled out of their chairs and followed. They'd been waiting for more than an hour to see the investigative reporter.

As Nikki hurried along behind the receptionist she read aloud the words on the doors on either side of the hallway. "Studio One . . . Studio Two . . . Editing . . . Wardrobe . . . Dressing Room . . . Makeup."

"Ohhh, I'd love to go in *that* door," Carrie said

with a sigh, pausing in front of the door that said MAKEUP.

Ben grabbed her by the sleeve and pulled her along. "C'mon. This is business."

The receptionist stopped in front of a door marked NEWS. "Here we are," she said, opening the door, then standing to one side.

The four friends walked into a noisy, brightly lit room full of desks, computers, and telex machines. It sounded as though a hundred typewriters were all going at once. Out of the commotion stepped a tall woman with short, curly hair and glasses.

"Welcome to WAPG," Julia Forbes said, smiling. "Sorry to have kept you sitting here, but I had a late-breaking story that couldn't wait." Julia turned and started walking across the room. "Come over to my desk and tell me what's going on."

At the newscaster's desk, Ben told her what the gang had seen at the carousel.

When he finished, Julia Forbes crossed her arms and leaned back in her chair. "That's quite a story. But I'm afraid it's rather hard to believe. Ghost riders? Carousel thieves? Are you sure it wasn't just shadows playing tricks on you? I'm afraid I need more evidence before I can do a story on it."

"I've got evidence," Ben cried. "I've got proof!" He reached into his pocket and pulled out the photographs. "Look at these."

"This will help," Nikki said, pulling her gadget with the retractable magnifying glass out of her pocket.

Using the glass, Julia Forbes looked at the photographs she had spread out on her desk. "Hmmm," she said. "Yes, I see. Hmmm. Yes." She looked up at Ben. "You took these photos?"

"I sure did," Ben answered. He nodded to his friends. "And they watched it all from the bushes."

"Well, it does look pretty strange, I must admit." She held up a photo. "And because of these, I think it deserves to be investigated." She picked up the phone. "I'll call my friend Officer Osgood at the police station and see what he thinks. If it is a real horse thief we're dealing with, he should know about it."

Julie called Officer Osgood and repeated the story to him on the phone. She paused, listening to his answer. Then she nodded. "Tonight?" She paused again. "Yes, tonight is fine for me. I'll tell them. Good-bye, now." She hung up the phone.

"Officer Osgood is coming right over to see the photographs," Julia Forbes said to the gang. "If he agrees that they're evidence enough to go on, he wants to stake out the carousel tonight. I'll come, too. If the thief shows up, I'll get it all on video for my show. I'll operate the camera myself—the fewer people involved, the better. But we'll need you kids to show us where to go."

"Sure thing!" Ben said excitedly.

In a very short time, Officer Osgood arrived at Julia Forbes's office. He studied Ben's photos with Nikki's magnifying glass.

"I'll admit this looks like pretty good evidence," he said. He turned to the gang. "But if this is just a prank, I can tell you right now that the police don't look kindly on wasting their time with such matters."

"It's not a prank, Officer Osgood," Ben said. "I promise." Nikki, Davey, and Carrie shook their heads in agreement.

Julia Forbes stood up. "Okay, kids. Tonight's the night. Officer Osgood and I will meet you at the park entrance just after sunset."

Ben's stomach felt as if it were full of butterflies as the kids left Julia Forbes's office. He'd never helped catch a real thief before. What if the thief got nasty? What if someone got hurt? Suddenly he felt scared. Really scared.

A few hours later, Ben scrambled along the twisting bike path toward the carousel, followed closely by the rest of the gang. Julia Forbes, with a camera slung over her shoulder, came next, and Officer Osgood brought up the rear.

I sure hope the thief comes tonight, Ben thought as he spotted the opening. *It'll be pretty embarrass-*

ing getting the police and Julia Forbes out here if nothing happens.

"This is it," Ben said, stopping at the now-familiar bushes. He pointed. "There's the carousel. The thief came out from the other side, where those shadows are."

"It's beautiful in the moonlight," Julia Forbes whispered. "I should get some great footage . . . if something happens." She looked around. "I need to move a few feet closer, but I'll stay in the shadow of the bushes so I can't be seen," she said to Officer Osgood, stepping out into the edge of the clearing.

"Be careful, Julia," the policeman whispered. He turned to the Apple Park Gang. "I want you kids to stay behind these bushes at all times. I don't want to risk anyone getting hurt. Just listen carefully and keep your eyes open." Then he stepped into a shadow and nearly disappeared into the night. The only sign of Officer Osgood was a glint of silver from the handcuffs hanging off his belt.

Everyone waited and watched. No one moved a muscle. *I'm glad it's a full moon,* Ben thought. *It'll be easy to spot the thief—if he comes.*

After about ten minutes, Ben was convinced the thief was taking the night off. Then he felt a sharp jab in his back.

"Look!" Carrie whispered. She pointed across the clearing.

Out of the shadows next to the carousel emerged the man with the black moustache. He looked from one side to the other, then jumped up onto the carousel.

Julia Forbes switched on the camera.

Officer Osgood felt for his handcuffs.

The Apple Park Gang held their breath.

The thief wove his way between the horses until he came to an old broken-down one. He stopped, pulled a large wrench from his pocket, unscrewed the horse, and set it by his feet.

"Bet he whistles with his fingers next, like last time," Nikki whispered.

The words were hardly out of her mouth before a short, sharp whistle cut through the silence. A smaller figure carrying a large object appeared from out of the shadows.

"Bet it's a new horse," Davey whispered.

The tall man took the object. As he turned into the moonlight, Ben muttered, "Right again."

Within seconds, the new, shiny carousel horse was galloping in place of the old one.

The man with the moustache smacked his hands together, laughed, and patted his short partner on the back. He picked up the old horse and was about to step down from the carousel when a deep, loud voice boomed out of the darkness.

"Put your hands up!"

Both thieves shot their arms straight up into the air.

Officer Osgood leaped onto the carousel and quickly clamped the handcuffs on the man with the moustache. He grabbed the short partner by the collar and pushed the two thieves to the edge of the carousel. "Let's get a good look at you two."

Julia Forbes was now standing only a couple of feet away, her camera focused on the two guilty-looking faces. Right behind her, lined up in a row, was the Apple Park Gang.

Ben recognized the man with the moustache right away in the light from Julia's camera. It was the man in his photographs—Big Jake, a known thief around Appleby Corners. But when the gang realized who the other thief was, they all let out a loud gasp.

"Wheels!" they yelled in unison.

"You know this rascal?" asked Officer Osgood.

"We sure do!" Ben answered. "It's Wheels Gilligan. He goes to our school!"

Carrie marched up to Wheels, hands on hips, and stuck her nose in his face. "What are you stealing carousel horses for?"

"None of your business," Wheels snarled.

"Here's the thief we want the answers from," Officer Osgood said, turning to Big Jake. You may as well spill the beans, Jake, 'cause we've got it all down on videotape." He turned and winked at Ben. "And in photographs, too."

At first Big Jake wouldn't cooperate, but

when he realized that Julia Forbes had just videotaped the whole theft, he confessed everything. His plan, he said, was to substitute all the old wooden carousel horses with shiny new plastic ones.

Ben was confused. "Why would he do that? Who would want a bunch of broken-down horses?"

Big Jake snorted. "To you they're broken-down horses. To a collector, they're expensive antiques."

"So you had someone lined up to buy the wooden horses?" Officer Osgood asked.

"Brilliant deduction, Osgood," Big Jake said with a sneer.

Officer Osgood turned to Wheels and gently squeezed his shoulder. "What did you have to do with all this, son?" he asked.

Wheels shrugged and didn't answer.

"It's not his fault," Big Jake said. "He didn't really know what was going on."

Big Jake explained how he'd hired Wheels to paint the new plastic horses and help him make the nighttime switch. "He thought the new horses were better than the old broken ones," Big Jake said with a laugh. "I told him we were doing the park a favor! I also told him not to tell anyone or he'd lose his job."

Officer Osgood shook his head slowly. "You should be ashamed of yourself, tricking a young kid like that."

"I guess you're right," Big Jake said, looking a little embarrassed.

"You've got some explaining to do, Jake," Officer Osgood said. "But right now I'm more interested in getting you down to the police station and Wheels back home. Let's go, you two."

The three jumped down from the carousel and started walking toward the path leading out of the park.

"Wait!" yelled Ben. "Look!"

From out of the shadows stepped the figure with the big hat and the long, flowing scarf.

"The ghost rider!" the gang murmured in one voice.

When she saw the group of people, the ghostly figure paused for a moment. Then, before anyone knew what was happening, she marched straight over to Big Jake—and hit him on the head with her umbrella. "Horse thief!" she yelled.

Officer Osgood grabbed the umbrella and held the ghost rider by the wrist.

"Let me go," she cried. "Let me go this instant!" In the tussle, the ghost rider's hat flew off.

"Mrs. Merrylegs!" cried Ben, Nikki, Davey, and Carrie.

"You know her, too?" Officer Osgood asked in amazement.

"Of course!" Davey answered. "Everyone knows

Mrs. Merrylegs. She's been coming to the park since before any of us were born."

The policeman gently released the old lady. Mrs. Merrylegs straightened out her dress. She picked up her hat and put it on. "So they've caught you at last, you scalawag," she said, wagging her finger at Big Jake. "That'll teach you to mess with my carousel."

"Your carousel?" asked the policeman.

"I've been riding that carousel since I was a little girl. It isn't used much anymore because no one will fix it up." Mrs. Merrylegs pointed at Big Jake. "One night I caught him switching the horses, so I decided to ride the carousel every night to try and stop him."

Ben stepped up to Mrs. Merrylegs. "If you hadn't ridden the carousel at night, we wouldn't have heard the ghostly music or caught Big Jake. You helped save the carousel, Mrs. Merrylegs."

Officer Osgood turned to the Apple Park Gang. "And so did you kids. You've done good work." He rested his hand on the old lady's shoulder. "Don't worry anymore about your carousel. We'll get all the old horses back, right where they belong."

"Wow! That was quite a story," exclaimed Julia Forbes, whose camera had been running the whole time. "It's going to be my lead item on the news tomorrow night. And guess what my second item will be?"

Everyone looked puzzled.

"The First Annual Apple Park Day Party!"

Nikki groaned. "Oh, no. With everything that's been going on, I completely forgot!"

"Well, now that we've caught the thieves, you've got one whole night to think of something," Carrie said. Everyone laughed.

"That better be enough time," Nikki said, her smile fading. "Otherwise, I'm going to be the only one with nothing to do!"

CHAPTER
SEVEN

The next day, the park was bustling with people. Gaily colored banners waved from tree branches and red, white, and blue balloons bobbed on the ends of strings tied to baby carriages and children's wrists. It looked like Apple Park Day was going to be a success.

Ben carefully guided a wheelbarrow full of costumes and his fully loaded camera through the crowds past his uncle's hot dog stand. "Frank's Franks" was printed in big red letters above the stand. There was such a long line of people waiting to be served that his uncle barely had time to wave when Ben called out, "Hey, Uncle Frank. How's it going?"

Ben grinned and continued past the lake. The gang had decided to set up their booths near the playground, where there would be lots of kids wanting their faces painted and their pictures taken.

"We were right," he said to himself as he neared the playground. There were so many people he could hardly move.

"Ben! Over here!" shouted Carrie. She was painting a little girl's face to look like a Raggedy Ann doll. Carrie had painted her own face like a smiling clown, and she was wearing a baggy clown outfit. At least a dozen kids were lined up under her sign, CARRIE'S CREATIONS.

"Hey, Carrie," Ben yelled. "How's business?"

"Great!" Carrie called. "Hurry and set up your booth. These kids want their pictures taken in their new faces!"

Ben dumped the pile of dress-up costumes on the ground beside Carrie's booth. "Have you seen Davey and Nikki? Did Nikki think of something to do?"

"Look!" Carrie pointed to a crowd of people. On a stepladder, above the crowd, sat Nikki. She was wearing a long black robe and a flat-topped black hat with a tassel hanging from one side. She looked like a professor. On her lap was a red tin can.

Ben pushed his way through the crowd. "What are you doing?" he called up to her.

Nikki grinned and pointed to a sign over her head: PROFESSOR NIKKI'S NOODLE NUDGERS.

Ben scratched his head. "What's a noodle nudger?"

"It's a brain teaser. Each one is like a little mystery. I got the idea last night when I was thinking about how we solved the mystery of the carousel."

Nikki reached into the can and grabbed a bunch of folded pieces of paper. "I've written a brain teaser on each of these. For ten cents, you can try to solve one. I'll give you five minutes, and if you solve the first one, the second one is free. If you solve the second one, you get your ten cents back. Want to try?"

Before Ben could answer, a loud and familiar voice behind him boomed, "Gimme one of those noodle nudgers. I can figure out anything."

It was Wheels.

Nikki stuck her hand out, palm side up, "Ten cents first, Wheels."

Grumbling, Wheels dug his hand into his pocket and pulled out a dime. He reached up and put it in Nikki's hand. Nikki held out the tin of noodle nudgers and let Wheels pick one.

"You have five minutes to figure it out," Nikki said. "Starting *now*." She pressed a button on

her calculator–compass–watch–stopwatch–alarm clock–magnifying glass.

Wheels opened the piece of paper and read out loud: "A man went outside. It was raining. He didn't wear a hat. He didn't carry an umbrella. His coat got wet. His pants got wet. His shoes got wet. But his hair didn't get wet. Why?"

Wheels wrinkled his brow. "This is dumb. Gimme my dime back."

"It's not dumb. There's a logical answer if you just think about it," Nikki said. "Want to try another one, Wheels?" she asked teasingly.

Ben smiled at Wheels. "Maybe you should quit before you lose any more money."

"I never quit!" Wheels snarled. "Give me another!" He pulled a dime from his pocket and tossed it to Nikki. Then he grabbed another noodle nudger. This time he read it to himself. Then, without a word, he crumpled the paper into a small ball, threw it onto the ground, and stomped off.

Nikki and Ben burst out laughing.

Ben picked up the paper ball, smoothed it out and read, "A waitress unwrapped a lump of sugar. She dropped it into her coffee. The sugar didn't get wet. Why not?"

Ben shook his head. "Pretty tricky, Nikki," he said. "I might be able to figure it out if I had time." He started back toward Carrie. "But if I don't get my booth set up soon, I won't make any money and I won't be able to pay my dad back. See you later."

"I'll tell you the answers at the end of the day," Nikki yelled after him.

The costumes were still on the ground, right where Ben had dumped them. He quickly sorted through them so his customers could choose what they wanted to wear when they had their photographs taken. No sooner had he arranged the costumes in small piles than he heard a familiar voice.

"Got any cowboy outfits?" It was Mike Morrissey. Max stood next to him. Carrie had painted their faces to look like rough-and-ready bandits. Mike had a big droopy moustache and thick black eyebrows. Max had two missing front teeth and a long scar running down one side of his face.

Ben laughed. "Sure thing, guys." He put ten-gallon hats on their heads and buckled toy guns in holsters around their waists.

The twins grinned and gave Ben a dollar. They stood perfectly still while he snapped the shutter.

"It'll take a minute to develop," Ben said, tearing off the shiny white paper and handing the photo to Max. "Thanks, guys."

"Look!" Mike cried. "The world's one and only singing dog!" He pointed to a crowd gathered around a huge cardboard box. The box was much taller than Ben. Along the top, in large black letters, was written REFRIGERATOR THIS END UP. Underneath was a picture of a howling dog surrounded by musical notes and the words, PITIFUL—THE KING OF ROCK 'N' ROLL!

"I'll be right back to take more photos," Ben called to Carrie, who still had a long line of kids waiting to be painted. "I've got to see this."

As Ben approached the crowd, he could hear Elvis singing "Hound Dog." Even louder, he could hear Pitiful howling.

"Hi, Davey," Ben called. "How's it going?"

"Great!" Davey answered. "Step inside and hear for yourself." Davey led Ben to the REFRIGERATOR THIS END UP box and carefully opened the cardboard cutout door. They both stepped inside. On the ground was Carrie's screaming yellow boom box, playing "Hound Dog." Pitiful lay beside it on his back, with his paws stretched straight up in the air. Tied onto his head was a small crown; a rhinestone necklace hung around the folds of his neck. Pitiful's eyes were closed, and he was howling loudly and pitifully.

Davey and Ben listened for a minute, then Davey shut off the music. Immediately, Pitiful flopped back onto his stomach, tucked his four short legs under his body, and went to sleep.

Davey jangled coins in his pocket. "I'm making lots of money," he said, "but I never want to hear Elvis again as long as I live." He laughed and added, "Or Pitiful, either!"

Ben raised his eyebrows. "I know what you mean! Well, I've gotta get back to my booth."

All the rest of the day, Ben photographed, Carrie painted, Nikki teased brains, and Pitiful howled along with Elvis. The sun was beginning to set when the Apple Park Gang, their pockets full of hard-earned cash, closed their booths and started making their weary way toward the entrance gate. They had not gotten far when they ran into Mr. P.

"Closing up shop?" he asked. "Did you have fun?"

"Sure did," Ben said. "It was a great park party."

"I was so busy that I never got to your booths," Mr. P said. "I wanted to thank you for getting the boats repaired on time. People used them all day. Oh, by the way, I heard what's been happening at the carousel from my old friend Officer Osgood. He told me that the original horses will be returned—and Wheels has to help repair them. He's lucky that's his only punishment."

"Mrs. Merrylegs will be happy," Nikki said. "She loves that old carousel."

"If it hadn't been for her, the thieves might have gotten away," Davey added.

"All's well that ends well," said Mr. P. "Well, I have to get going. I've got to make sure everything is in order in the park before I close the gates." He disappeared along the path that led through the park.

"Hey, Nikki," Ben asked. "Did anyone figure out your brain teasers?"

"Just one or two people," Nikki answered. "Now that the party is over, I'll tell you the answers."

Nikki repeated the two riddles that had stumped Wheels. "The answer to the first one about the man going for a walk in the rain but not getting his hair wet is . . . the man didn't have any hair. He was bald!"

"Why didn't I think of that?" Ben said, snapping his fingers.

"That's pretty clever," Carrie said. "I could have thought for a million years and never figured it out."

"I bet the sugar and coffee one is easy, too— once you know the answer," Davey said.

Nikki grinned. "The waitress put the sugar cube into—are you ready for this, Davey?—into a can of coffee beans!"

"Enough! Enough!" yelled Carrie, clutching her head with both hands. "I can't stand any more riddles. Let's get out of here."

With Carrie in the lead, the gang made their way to the park entrance. A large van with the letters WAPG on the side was parked just outside the gate.

"There's Julia Forbes!" Carrie shouted, pointing to the reporter.

When Julia Forbes heard her name, she turned around and walked over to the gang. "Hi, kids. Did you enjoy the party?"

"Sure did," Nikki answered. "Were you covering it for your show?"

"You bet. It'll follow my lead story about the carousel." She turned to Ben. "I still have your photos that you took in the moonlight. Can I keep them another day?"

"Sure, but what for?" Ben asked.

"Watch my show tonight. You'll see," she answered mysteriously. Julia Forbes glanced at her watch. "I've got to run. Just an hour before I'm on the air. Don't forget to watch."

Ben and his parents turned on the TV in their living room and waited for the Julia Forbes Report to begin.

"Your Uncle Frank told me he did more business today than he's ever done before," Mr. Ferber said. "How did your photography go, son?"

"Great! I made enough money to buy—"

Ben didn't have time to finish his sentence. Julia Forbes was on the air. In the upper right-hand corner of the screen was a picture of the carousel. In front of the carousel was a sign that said, UNDER REPAIR. DO NOT RIDE UNTIL FURTHER NOTICE.

Julia spoke. "Good evening. Our lead story tonight features a talented young photographer whose photos helped capture a pair of horse thieves in Apple Park. His name is Ben Ferber, and here's one of his photos."

Ben gasped. There on the screen was his "artistic" photograph of Mrs. Merrylegs riding the carousel in the moonlight!

"I hope we'll be seeing more of this young man's work," Julia went on. "Now here's the story of the horse thieves."

Ben and his parents watched silently as Julia Forbes ran her video of Big Jake and Wheels switching the horses at the carousel.

When it was over, Mr. Ferber let out a long whistle. "So, that's what all that moonlight photography was about. You were capturing horse thieves!"

"Me and my friends and Julia Forbes and Officer Osgood," Ben said, nodding his head.

Mrs. Ferber put her arm around Ben's shoulder. "We're very proud of you, son."

"And do you know what I'm going to do?" Ben's father smiled.

"What?" asked Ben.

"I'm going to forget about that loan I gave you to buy film. Consider it a present."

Ben smiled. He picked up his camera from the table. "Thanks, Dad. Now, do you know what I'm going to do for you two?"

"No, Ben, what?" his mother asked.

"I'm going to take your picture! Say 'Cheese'!"